## TIPS FOR READING TO TODDLERS

Here are some ways to get the most out of reading *Tomie dePaola's Mother Goose*
and other books with your toddler:

- When you read together, cuddle up with your child on your lap. Remember to look at each other as well as the book.

- Let your child lead. Since this is a collection of nursery rhymes it will be very easy to skip ahead and go forward and backwards through the book as your child wants to. If your child wants to read the same rhymes again and again, it's okay.

- Point out things in the pictures to your child. For instance, ask "Do you see the crooked house?" and have your child find it on the page.

- Ask your child to name things in the pictures and talk about them. In the rhyme, "Old Mother Hubbard," ask your child "What is this?" as you point to the various food items Mother Hubbard brings home for the dog to eat. After each item, ask your child, "Do you like to eat that?"

- Use the pictures to teach new words. Say, "See the beehive? A beehive is a house for bees. They make honey inside of it, which is something sweet that we can eat." or "See the haystack? A haystack is a large pile of hay which farmers use to feed animals like cows and horses. It is made from stalks of grass that are cut down."

- Use the story to start a conversation. If it is raining outside, start to sing. "Rain rain, go away. Come again another day." Talk to your child about what things they can do when it is raining and how those things are different from what they can do when it is not raining.

- Ask questions about a rhyme. "What is Little Boy Blue doing under the haystack?" Pause and then help your child answer. Allow your child to make things up.

- Act out parts of the rhyme. In Little Bo Peep, when you read "wagging their tails behind them," wag your bottom.

Here are some ways you can extend your toddler's learning "on the go":

- Bring books to read while you wait in line at the market or at the doctor's office.

- Talk about books you've read when you are at the park or on a walk. "Look! There are a lot of birds like the ones that were baked in the pie. Did those birds sing when the pie was cut open?"

- Use a word or phrase from a story throughout the day. For example, as you buckle or tie your child's shoes say, "One, two, buckle my shoe. Three, four, shut the door."

# Tomie dePaola's
# MOTHER GOOSE

G. P. Putnam's Sons
An Imprint of Penguin Group (USA) Inc.

*For all my friends in my old hometown,
Meriden, Connecticut*

Wherever possible, the Mother Goose rhymes in this book
are the classic versions collected by Peter and Iona Opie.

G. P. PUTNAM'S SONS
A division of Penguin Young Readers Group. Published by The Penguin Group.
Penguin Group (USA) Inc., 375 Hudson Street, New York, NY 10014, U.S.A.
Penguin Group (Canada), 90 Eglinton Avenue East, Suite 700, Toronto, Ontario M4P 2Y3, Canada
(a division of Pearson Penguin Canada Inc.).
Penguin Books Ltd, 80 Strand, London WC2R 0RL, England.
Penguin Ireland, 25 St. Stephen's Green, Dublin 2, Ireland (a division of Penguin Books Ltd.).
Penguin Group (Australia), 250 Camberwell Road, Camberwell, Victoria 3124, Australia (a division of Pearson Australia Group Pty Ltd).
Penguin Books India Pvt Ltd, 11 Community Centre, Panchsheel Park, New Delhi - 110 017, India.
Penguin Group (NZ), 67 Apollo Drive, Rosedale, North Shore 0632, New Zealand (a division of Pearson New Zealand Ltd).
Penguin Books (South Africa) (Pty) Ltd, 24 Sturdee Avenue, Rosebank, Johannesburg 2196, South Africa.
Penguin Books Ltd, Registered Offices: 80 Strand, London WC2R 0RL, England.

Manufactured in China by South China Printing Co. Ltd.
Jacket design by Marikka Tamura.
ISBN 978-0-399-21258-1
Special Markets ISBN 978-0-399-25564-9 Not for resale
3  5  7  9  10  8  6  4  2

This Imagination Library edition is published by Penguin Group (USA), a Pearson
company, exclusively for Dolly Parton's Imagination Library, a not-for-profit
program designed to inspire a love of reading and learning, sponsored in part by The
Dollywood Foundation. Penguin's trade editions of this work are available wherever
books are sold.

This Book Belongs To

_____

Old Mother Goose,
     When she wanted to wander,
Would ride through the air
     On a very fine gander.

Mother Goose had a house,
     'Twas built in a wood,
Where an owl at the door
     For sentinel stood.

She had a son Jack,
     A plain-looking lad,
He was not very good,
     Nor yet very bad.

She sent him to market,
     A live goose he bought;
See, mother, says he,
     I have not been for nought.

Jack's goose and her gander
     Grew very fond;
They'd both eat together,
     Or swim in the pond.

Jack found one fine morning,
    As I have been told,
His goose had laid him
    An egg of pure gold.

Jack ran to his mother
    The news for to tell,
She called him a good boy,
    And said it was well.

Jack sold his gold egg
    To a merchant untrue,
Who cheated him out of
    A half of his due.

Then Jack went a-courting
    A lady so gay,
As fair as the lily,
    And sweet as the May.

The merchant and squire
    Soon came at his back,
And began to belabour
    The sides of poor Jack.

Then old Mother Goose
    That instant came in,
And turned her son Jack
    Into famed Harlequin.

She then with her wand
    Touched the lady so fine,
And turned her at once
    Into sweet Columbine.

The gold egg in the sea
    Was thrown away then,
When an odd fish brought her
    The egg back again.

The merchant then vowed
    The goose he would kill,
Resolving at once
    His pockets to fill.

Jack's mother came in,
    And caught the goose soon,
And mounting its back,
    Flew up to the moon.

Pussy cat, pussy cat,
    Where have you been?
I've been to London
    To look at the Queen.
Pussy cat, pussy cat,
    What did you there?
I frightened a little mouse
    Under her chair.

A diller, a dollar,
A ten o'clock scholar,
What makes you come so soon?
You used to come at ten o'clock,
But now you come at noon.

I saw a ship a-sailing,
A-sailing on the sea;
And, oh! it was all laden
With pretty things for thee!

There were comfits in the cabin,
And apples in the hold;
The sails were made of silk,
And the masts were made of gold.

The four-and-twenty sailors
That stood between the decks,
Were four-and-twenty white mice
With chains about their necks.

The captain was a duck,
With a packet on his back;
And when the ship began to move,
The captain said, "Quack! Quack!"

Lavender's blue, diddle, diddle,
  Lavender's green;
When I am king, diddle, diddle,
  You shall be queen.

Call up your men, diddle, diddle,
  Set them to work,
Some to the plough, diddle, diddle,
  Some to the cart.

Some to make hay, diddle, diddle,
  Some to thresh corn,
Whilst you and I, diddle, diddle,
  Keep ourselves warm.

Sing a song of sixpence,
 A pocket full of rye;
Four and twenty blackbirds,
 Baked in a pie.

When the pie was opened,
 The birds began to sing;
Was not that a dainty dish,
 To set before a king?

The king was in his counting-house,
 Counting out his money;
The queen was in the parlour
 Eating bread and honey.

The maid was in the garden,
 Hanging out the clothes,
When down came a blackbird
 And pecked off her nose.

Old woman, old woman,
    Shall we go a-shearing?
Speak a little louder, sir,
    I'm very thick of hearing.
Old woman, old woman,
    Shall I love you dearly?
Thank you very kindly, sir,
    Now I hear you clearly.

Tweedledum and Tweedledee
    Agreed to have a battle,
For Tweedledum said Tweedledee
    Had spoiled his nice new rattle.
Just then flew by a monstrous crow
    As black as a tar-barrel,
Which frightened both the heroes so,
    They quite forgot their quarrel.

Dickery, dickery, dare,
The pig flew up in the air;
The man in brown
Soon brought him down,
Dickery, dickery, dare.

Little Poll Parrot
Sat in his garret
Eating toast and tea;
A little brown mouse
Jumped into the house
And stole it all away.

When I was a little boy
    I lived by myself,
And all the bread and cheese I got
    I laid upon a shelf.

The rats and the mice
    They made such a strife,
I had to go to London town
    And get me a wife.

The streets were so broad
    And the lanes were so narrow,
I was forced to bring my wife home
    In a wheelbarrow.

The wheelbarrow broke
    And my wife had a fall,
Farewell wheelbarrow,
    Little wife and all.

Bobby Shaftoe's gone to sea,
Silver buckles at his knee;
He'll come back and marry me,
    Bonny Bobby Shaftoe.

Bobby Shaftoe's bright and fair,
Combing down his yellow hair,
He's my ain for evermair,
    Bonny Bobby Shaftoe.

Bobby Shaftoe's tall and slim,
He's always dressed so neat and trim,
The ladies they all keek at him,
    Bonny Bobby Shaftoe.

Bobby Shaftoe's getten a bairn
For to dandle in his arm;
In his arm and on his knee,
    Bobby Shaftoe loves me.

The north wind doth blow,
And we shall have snow,
And what will poor Robin do then,
    Poor thing?
He'll sit in a barn,
And keep himself warm,
And hide his head under his wing,
    Poor thing.

Rain before seven,
Fine before eleven.

Rain, rain, go away,
Come again another day,
Little Johnny wants to play.
Rain, rain, go to Spain,
Never show your face again.

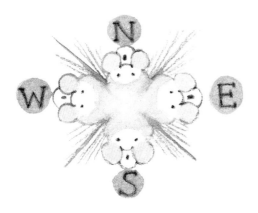

When the wind is in the east,
'Tis neither good for man nor beast;
When the wind is in the north,
The skilful fisher goes not forth;
When the wind is in the south,
It blows the bait in the fishes' mouth;
When the wind is in the west,
Then 'tis at the very best.

March winds and April showers
Bring forth May flowers.

Red sky at night,
Shepherd's delight;
Red sky in the morning,
Shepherd's warning.

If bees stay at home,
Rain will soon come;
If they fly away,
Fine will be the day.

A sunshiny shower
Won't last half an hour.

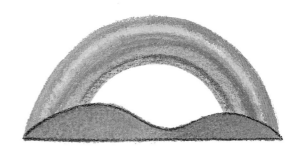

Rain on the green grass,
  And rain on the tree,
Rain on the house-top,
  But not on me.

It's raining, it's pouring,
The old man's snoring;
He got into bed
And bumped his head
And couldn't get up in the morning.

Cold and raw the north wind doth blow,
Bleak in the morning early;
All the hills are covered with snow,
And winter's now come fairly.

Blow, wind, blow!
And go, mill, go!
That the miller may grind his corn;
That the baker may take it,
And into bread make it,
And bring us a loaf in the morn.

Old Mother Hubbard
Went to the cupboard,
To fetch her poor dog a bone;
But when she got there
The cupboard was bare
And so the poor dog had none.

She went to the baker's
To buy him some bread;
But when she came back
The poor dog was dead.

She went to the undertaker's
To buy him a coffin;
But when she came back
The poor dog was laughing.

She took a clean dish
To get him some tripe;
But when she came back
He was smoking a pipe.

She went to the fishmonger's
To buy him some fish;
But when she came back
He was licking the dish.

She went to the tavern
For white wine and red;
But when she came back
The dog stood on his head.

She went to the fruiterer's
To buy him some fruit;
But when she came back
He was playing the flute.

She went to the tailor's
    To buy him a coat;
But when she came back
    He was riding a goat.

She went to the hatter's
    To buy him a hat;
But when she came back
    He was feeding the cat.

She went to the barber's
    To buy him a wig;
But when she came back
    He was dancing a jig.

She went to the cobbler's
    To buy him some shoes;
But when she came back
    He was reading the news.

She went to the seamstress
    To buy him some linen;
But when she came back
    The dog was a-spinning.

She went to the hosier's
    To buy him some hose;
But when she came back
    He was dressed in his clothes.

The dame made a curtsey,
    The dog made a bow;
The dame said, Your Servant,
    The dog said, Bow-bow.

There was a crooked man,
   And he walked a crooked mile,
He found a crooked sixpence
   Against a crooked stile;
He bought a crooked cat,
   Which caught a crooked mouse,
And they all lived together
   In a little crooked house.

Little Boy Blue,
　　Come blow your horn,
The sheep's in the meadow,
　　The cow's in the corn.
Where is the boy
　　Who looks after the sheep?
He's under a haystack,
　　Fast asleep.
Will you wake him?
　　No, not I,
For if I do,
　　He's sure to cry.

There came an old woman from
    France
Who taught grown-up children to
    dance;
    But they were so stiff,
    She sent them home in a sniff,
This sprightly old woman from
    France.

Three wise men of Gotham
Went to sea in a bowl
If the bowl had been stronger,
My story would have been longer.

Ride a cock-horse to Banbury Cross,
To see a fine lady upon a white horse;
Rings on her fingers and bells on her toes,
And she shall have music wherever she goes.

Taffy was a Welshman,
 Taffy was a thief,
Taffy came to my house
 And stole a piece of beef.

I went to Taffy's house,
 Taffy wasn't in,
I jumped upon his Sunday hat
 And poked it with a pin.

Taffy was a Welshman,
 Taffy was a sham,
Taffy came to my house
 And stole a leg of lamb.

I went to Taffy's house,
 Taffy was not there,
I hung his coat and trousers
 To roast before a fire.

Taffy was a Welshman,
 Taffy was a cheat,
Taffy came to my house
 And stole a piece of meat.

I went to Taffy's house,
 Taffy wasn't home;
Taffy came to my house
 And stole a marrow bone.

Ladies and gentlemen come to
supper—
Hot boiled beans and very good
butter.

Hush, baby, my dolly, I pray you
don't cry,
And I'll give you some bread, and
some milk by-and-by;
Or perhaps you like custard, or,
maybe a tart,
Then to either you're welcome, with
all my heart.

Molly, my sister, and I fell out,
And what do you think it was all about?
She loved coffee and I loved tea,
And that was the reason we couldn't agree.

Jack Sprat could eat no fat,
  His wife could eat no lean,
And so between them both, you see,
  They licked the platter clean.

Little Tommy Tucker
  Sings for his supper:
What shall we give him?
  White bread and butter.
How shall he cut it
  Without e'er a knife?
How will he be married
  Without e'er a wife?

Polly put the kettle on,
Polly put the kettle on,
Polly put the kettle on,
  We'll all have tea.

Sukey take it off again,
Sukey take it off again,
Sukey take it off again,
  They've all gone away.

Simple Simon met a pieman
   Going to the fair;
Says Simple Simon to the pieman,
   Let me taste your ware.

Says the pieman to Simple Simon,
   Show me first your penny;
Says Simple Simon to the pieman,
   Indeed I have not any.

Simple Simon went a-fishing,
   For to catch a whale;
All the water he had got
   Was in his mother's pail.

He went to catch a dickey bird,
    And thought he could not fail,
Because he'd got a little salt,
    To put upon its tail.

Once Simon made a great snowball,
    And brought it in to roast;
He laid it down before the fire,
    And soon the ball was lost.

He went for water in a sieve,
    But soon it all ran through;
And now poor Simple Simon
    Bids you all adieu.

1, 2,
Buckle my shoe;

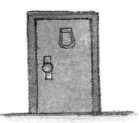

3, 4,
Knock at the door;

5, 6,
Pick up sticks;

7, 8,
Lay them straight;

9, 10,
A big fat hen;

11, 12,
Dig and delve;

13, 14,
Maids a-courting;

15, 16,
Maids in the kitchen;

17, 18,
Maids in waiting;

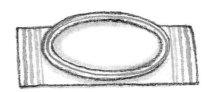

19, 20,
My plate's empty.

Little Bo-peep has lost her sheep,
    And doesn't know where to find them;
Leave them alone, and they'll come home,
    Bringing their tails behind them.

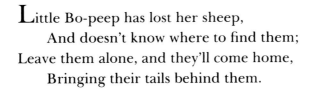

Little Bo-peep fell fast asleep,
    And dreamt she heard them bleating;
But when she awoke, she found it a joke,
    For they were still a-fleeting.

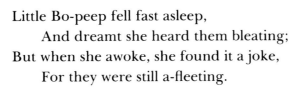

Then up she took her little crook,
    Determined for to find them;
She found them indeed, but it made her heart bleed
    For they'd left their tails behind them.

It happened one day, as Bo-peep did stray
    Into a meadow hard by,
There she espied their tails side by side,
    All hung on a tree to dry.

She heaved a sigh, and wiped her eye,
    And over the hillocks went rambling,
And tried what she could, as a shepherdess should,
    To tack again each to its lambkin.

High diddle doubt, my candle's out
My little maid is not at home;
Saddle my hog and bridle my dog,
And fetch my little maid home.

Dance, little Baby, dance up high!
Never mind, Baby, Mother is by.
Crow and caper, caper and crow,
There, little Baby, there you go!
Up to the ceiling, down to the
    ground,
Backwards and forwards, round
    and round;
Dance, little Baby and Mother
    will sing,
With the merry coral, ding, ding,
    ding!

"I went up one pair of stairs."
"Just like me."
"I went up two pairs of stairs."
"Just like me."
"I went into a room."
"Just like me."
"I looked out of a window."
"Just like me."
"And there I saw a monkey."
"Just like me."

To make your candles last for aye,
You wives and maids give ear-O!
To put them out's the only way,
Says honest John Boldero.

Jerry Hall,
He is so small,
A rat could eat him,
Hat and all.

Little girl, little girl,
    Where have you been?
I've been to see grandmother
    Over the green.
What did she give you?
    Milk in a can.
What did you say for it?
    Thank you, Grandam.

What are little boys made of, made of?
What are little boys made of?
    Frogs and snails
    And puppy-dogs' tails,
That's what little boys are made of.

What are little girls made of, made of?
What are little girls made of?
    Sugar and spice
    And all things nice,
That's what little girls are made of.

Old King Cole
Was a merry old soul,
And a merry old soul was he;
He called for his pipe,
And he called for his bowl,
And he called for his fiddlers three.

Every fiddler he had a fiddle,
And a very fine fiddle had he;
Oh, there's none so rare
As can compare
With King Cole and his fiddlers three.

Jack and Jill
Went up the hill,
To fetch a pail of water;
Jack fell down,
And broke his crown,
And Jill came tumbling after.

Then up Jack got,
And home did trot,
As fast as he could caper;
To old Dame Dob,
Who patched his nob
With vinegar and brown paper.

When Jill came in,
How she did grin
To see Jack's paper plaster;
Her mother, vexed,
Did whip her next,
For laughing at Jack's disaster.

Now Jack did laugh
And Jill did cry,
But her tears did soon abate;
Then Jill did say,
That they should play
At see-saw across the gate.

Goosey, goosey gander,
    Whither shall I wander?
Upstairs and downstairs
    And in my lady's chamber.
There I met an old man
    Who would not say his prayers,
I took him by the left leg
    And threw him down the stairs.

Hickety, pickety, my black hen,
She lays eggs for gentlemen;
Gentlemen come every day
To see what my black hen doth lay.